Disney · PIXAR

MONSTERS UNIVERSITY

STICKER SCENES

PaRragon

Bath · New York · Singapore · Hong Kong · Cologne · Delhi
Melbourne · Amsterdam · Johannesburg · Shenzhen

SCHOOL OF SCARING

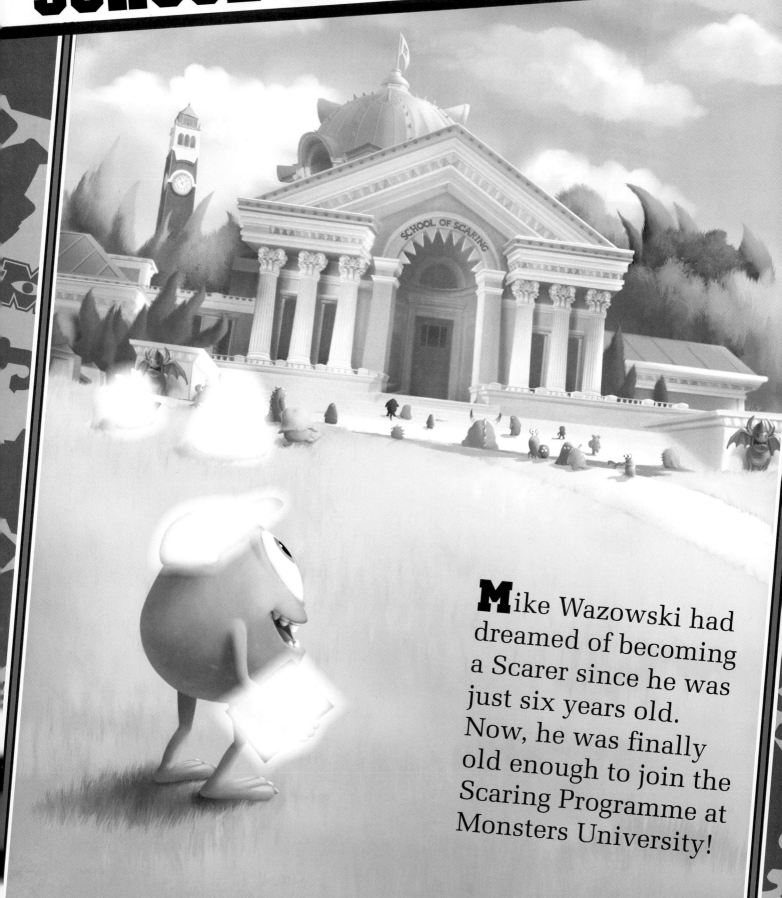

Mike Wazowski had dreamed of becoming a Scarer since he was just six years old. Now, he was finally old enough to join the Scaring Programme at Monsters University!

Mike studied very hard, but his classmate, Sulley, just messed around. One day, Mike and Sulley got into a big argument. They accidentally broke Dean Hardscrabble's special scream can. She kicked them both out of the Scaring Programme!

There was only one way that Mike and Sulley could get back into the Scaring Programme: win the annual Scare Games! To enter, they had to join a fraternity. The only students that would have them were a group of misfits called the Oozma Kappas.

STICK A MONSTERS UNIVERSITY BADGE HERE!

THE SCARE GAMES

For the first event, the teams had to avoid stinging glow urchins in a sewer tunnel. When the race started, Mike and Sulley took off and left the rest of their team behind! Oozma Kappa finished last.

MONSTERS, INC.

Luckily, the OKs got through to the next round. But they still weren't working together as a team. So, Mike decided to take everyone on a trip to Monsters, Inc., where professional Scarers worked. He showed them that the top Scarers were monsters of all shapes and sizes. The OKs were inspired!

SCHOOL OF SCARING

THE SCARE GAMES

THE SCARE GAMES

MONSTERS, INC.

WINNERS!

THE HUMAN WORLD

JUST THE BEGINNING

EXTRAS

MONSTERS

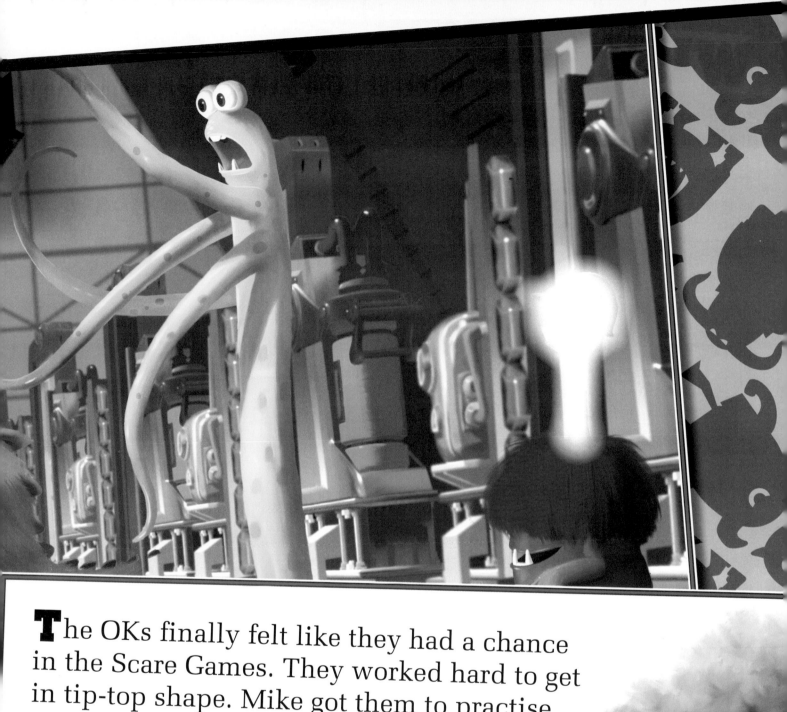

The OKs finally felt like they had a chance in the Scare Games. They worked hard to get in tip-top shape. Mike got them to practise their 'scary feet' for hours!

WINNERS!

The OKs did great in the next two Scare Game events. They got to the finals, where all the competitors had to scare a robot child. The Oozma Kappas won! They were back in the Scaring Programme!

But Mike found out that Sulley had fixed the final test because he didn't think Mike could pull off a big enough scare. The OKs hadn't really won. Mike was devastated.

THE HUMAN WORLD

Wanting to prove that he *could* be scary, Mike activated a door that led to a cabin in the human world. When he walked through the door, he tried to scare the children there. But the children just laughed when they saw him! Mike was sad. Luckily, Sulley came to find him and managed to get Mike back to the cabin.

Mike and Sulley needed a lot of scream power to get back through the door into the monster world. They worked together as a team to scare a whole group of human adults!

STICK YOUR MU FLAG HERE!

FIND A MONSTERS UNIVERSITY BADGE TO STICK HERE!

JUST THE BEGINNING

Back at the university, Mike and Sulley burst through the door. They had pulled off the biggest scare Monsters University had ever seen

Mike and Sulley ended up getting expelled from MU. But that didn't stop them from following their dreams. They got jobs in the mailroom at Monsters, Inc.! They knew that if they worked hard, anything was possible. This was just the beginning for Team Wazowski and Sullivan....